My Yeti Loves Spaghetti!

Book One

Hart Lee Serious

My Yeti Loves Spaghetti! Book One by Hart Lee Serious

* * *

Published by Picture Perfect Books, 2019

Chapter 1 – My Not-So-Little Secret

Okay, the first thing I have to tell you is that I have a secret. A really BIG secret! Literally—like, a seven-foot-tall secret. His name is Franklin, he's my best friend in the whole world, and he's a yeti with a serious pasta addiction.

And he hides under my bed.

Do you know what a yeti is? It's what some people call an *abominable snowman*. A shaggy monster that lives high up in the icy Himalaya Mountains. Some people think they are imaginary because they are hard to spot. But that's only because they're super fast, and they are white and hide easily against the snow.

Now, I know you're probably rolling your eyes and thinking, "Yeah, right! Who has a real yeti under their bed? A yeti that likes pasta? That's nuts!"

Well, I do. My name is Sam and I'm just a normal eight-year-old kid, but the way I met Franklin and how he came to live with us is anything *but* normal.

So let me tell you all about it.

Chapter 2 – The Night It Snowed Big Time

The night the big storm hit, I was scared to go to bed.

Just so you know, I'm not usually afraid of going to bed by myself. I'm in third grade. I'm a big boy, thank you very much. The dark doesn't frighten me, and I'm not bothered by strange noises either.

But the night my yeti showed up, the wind was howling outside like a pack of hungry wolves, and the branches of the trees in our yard were scratching against my bedroom window. It sounded like witches' claws dragging across glass.

On top of that, I could see the snow dancing around against the cloudy sky through my curtains, creating weird shapes and shadows. You bet I was spooked!

Mom had just tucked me in and kissed me goodnight, when I heard a loud tapping on my window, followed by a long, low moan. I thought I saw the curtains move. My heart almost jumped into my throat! So I threw off my covers and ran downstairs as fast as I could.

"Mom! Dad!" I shouted, racing into the living room where they were watching TV. "I heard a monster outside the house!"

"A monster, huh?" said Dad. "Then we better make sure he doesn't get into your room. Come on, Sam. We'll go back upstairs and I'll check things out."

Dad winked at Mom and took my hand, and together we returned to my bedroom. I was shaking as we approached my open door, but it wasn't just because I was scared—I was *cold!*

A freezing breeze whipped out of my room and sent shivers down my spine. Goosebumps popped up all over my arms. Dad pulled my door open wide and snow blasted our faces as a strong gust almost knocked us over.

My window, which I swear had been closed only minutes before, was now COMPLETELY OPEN!

Chapter 3 – The Last Place to Look

"Whoa!" said Dad, squinting and pushing against the icy air as it roared around us. "Sam, why did you leave your window open?"

He made his way to the window and slammed it shut, then put his hands on his hips and looked at me with a puzzled smile.

"I d-d-didn't!" I said, my teeth chattering. "It must have been the monster!"

"Hmmmmm," Dad replied, scratching his chin. "I don't think so. This is the biggest winter storm to hit our town in years, so it was probably just the wind you heard. And with such strong gales, you have to lock your windows, too. Otherwise they can blow open."

"So you don't think it was a monster?" I asked nervously.

Dad shook his head. "Definitely not."

"Will you look in my closet to make sure?" I said.

Dad nodded, then he checked my closet and peeked around the curtains, and looked behind my dresser for good measure. He even kicked the big pile of dirty clothes on the floor. I felt better after that, because I knew there definitely couldn't be anything scary in my room now.

Or so I thought.

Dad tucked me in again, and kissed me on the forehead, then he turned off the light and left. I listened to him padding downstairs while the breeze continued to howl outside, and I tried not to think about the way it sounded like creepy ghosts.

Then I heard it.

A tiny scraping noise against the wood on my floor, nothing like the branches on the glass outside. I gulped and clutched my covers to my nose, wishing it would go away, and for a moment it did.

Then it started again, slow and steady, followed by a shuffling sound and a tiny thump against my mattress.

The MONSTER!

I almost screamed right then and there, but I couldn't. I was frozen in panic, my voice strangled in my throat. I quaked under my sheets, then I frowned and decided I was being silly. Dad had said there wasn't a monster in my room, and I believed him. He had checked everywhere to make sure.

Except under my bed.

I gulped. To prove my father right, there was one last place to look. So I worked up the courage to throw my blanket off and put my feet on the floor, then I cautiously dropped to my knees and peeked beneath my mattress.

Chapter 4 – A Huge Discovery

There was nothing there.

I mean, there *was* lots of stuff under my bed, but it was mostly old toys, bits of plastic blocks, a couple of shoes, a few stinky socks, and a plate of unfinished spaghetti I had eaten as a snack after school. But no monster, and nothing unusual.

Except a tiny puddle of water.

I dipped my finger in it and smelled to see if it was something I spilled, maybe a glass of juice I had forgotten about. But it was only water. Clear, *cold* water.

Suddenly, I felt someone staring at me.

I grabbed the fork off my plate and stood, and as I did, a rush of air brushed my cheeks in the dark. The wind was still whistling outside, but my window was definitely shut.

I thought I saw movement on the other side of my bed, so I ducked down again to look under the mattress, then I jumped back up before I reached the floor.

And there he was, caught before he could crouch and avoid detection. A tall, skinny, hairy man, with big ears and large hands, and eyes that glowed green in the dim light. Melting ice crystals glittered on his white fur like diamonds. He was big, REALLY big, and I was sure I spotted a pair of sharp fangs gleaming in his savage smile.

A YETI!

This time I did scream, but it only came out like a chicken's squawk. How embarrassing is that? The yeti yelled too, but his voice was hoarse and it sounded like the whooshing air outside. He stumbled back against the wall, while I tripped and fell on my butt by the door.

"Don't hurt me!" I cried, holding out the fork like a sword as I raised my arm over my head and squeezed shut my eyes.

I gritted my teeth and waited for the monster to attack, but nothing happened. A minute passed, then I lowered my hands and peeked to see where he was.

"Don't hurt me!" the yeti hissed, copying my movements and cowering by the curtains. He was trembling. His face was wrinkled up in fear, and his eyes were wide with terror as he stared at the fork with noodles hanging off it.

I blinked, unsure if what I was seeing could be true. Here he was, a monster in my room who was three times my size, and *he* was afraid of *me!*

"Don't hurt me!" the yeti repeated, in a sad little whisper.

A tiny teardrop glistened at the corner of his eye, before it ran down his frosty blue cheek.

Chapter 5 – Meet and Eat

I almost laughed at what a crazy scene it was, except the yeti didn't find it funny. He was too busy quaking by the window, glancing at the fork still in my hand as he nervously licked his lips. He thought it was a weapon!

"Hey, it's okay. I'm not going to hurt you," I said softly, putting the utensil behind my back. I pointed to myself, then at him with my finger. "I'm Sam. Who are you?"

The yeti blinked.

"Frunklgn," he mumbled.

"Frunklgn?" I asked. "What kind of name is that?"

"Frunklgn!" he insisted, tapping his muscly chest.

"You mean, *Franklin?*" I smiled. "How about if I call you that? Is Franklin alright?"

The yeti nodded.

"How did you get here, Franklin?" I said. "You look like you're a long ways from home."

The yeti blinked again.

"Are you lost?" I guessed. "Were you running away from somebody?"

Franklin didn't reply, he just continued to stare at me with a sad expression while his nose twitched, sniffing the air. A rumble sounded from his belly, filling my room with an unhappy growl.

I rubbed my stomach and pointed to my mouth. "Are you hungry?"

"Hungry!" Franklin agreed, nodding enthusiastically and patting the fur on his tummy.

"Okay," I said. "I'll go get you some food, and then maybe you can tell me more about yourself. Don't go anywhere!"

I snuck downstairs and tried to tiptoe past the living room, but Dad heard my footsteps and stopped me before I reached the kitchen.

"What are you doing, Sam? You're supposed to be in bed!"

My brain raced as I tried to come up with a good story but I couldn't think of anything. So I decided to tell the truth. I knew he wouldn't believe me, but what was I supposed to say? Maybe if he thought I was joking, he wouldn't question me further.

"Dad, there *is* a monster in my room. A yeti! You didn't look under my bed where he was hiding. I think he's scared and hungry, so I need to get him a little snack."

"A yeti, huh?" grinned Dad, winking at Mom.

"That's right," I said.

"Well, he's a guest in our house," said Mom, to my surprise, "so I suppose we better show him some hospitality. You may take him a little food. But you still need to go to bed soon."

"I will!" I promised, hurrying to the kitchen to grab as much as I could carry.

I searched the cupboards and found a box of cereal, then grabbed some potato chips from the pantry and two apples out of the fruit basket on our table. I wasn't sure what yetis liked to eat, but it was a start.

Chapter 6 – Spaghetti for a Yeti

"Bleccchhh!" said Franklin, spitting out the apple with displeasure.

"You don't like fruit?" I asked. "Alright, then how about cereal?"

I handed the yeti my sugary corn flakes and he opened the box and poured them down his wide-open mouth. His cheeks puffed out as he crunched them with his teeth, then he made a funny face and spat them out like the fruit.

"Yarrrrrgghhhh!" he cried, shaking his shaggy head.

I frowned. "Well, maybe you'll enjoy potato chips."

Franklin took the chip bag from me and sniffed it suspiciously, then opened it and emptied it onto his big pink tongue.

"Fffffpppphhhhh!" he gagged, blowing little crumbs everywhere before he swallowed the first bite. His grabbed his stomach and moaned.

"Hungry!" he said, his eyes watering like he was going to cry again.

I raced downstairs and got more stuff. Some bananas, a loaf of bread, a jar of peanut butter, a stick of butter, a carton of milk, a can of chili, a pack of ham, a few oranges, and a bar of chocolate. I had to be extra quiet so my parents didn't hear, but I managed to make it back to my room with my arms full of new food.

But none of it was any good.

One after another, Franklin tried all the things I brought him, but he never took more than a few bites before he made animal grunting noises and spat it onto the floor.

I retrieved more food, and he rejected it. I went back again, and again, and again . . . and still it wasn't any use.

The more he grumbled unhappily, the more frustrated I got, until finally I ran out of ideas—as well as new items to fetch. With all the cartons, cans, and empty food wrappers scattered around, my bedroom was starting to look like a dumpster behind a supermarket!

"I'm sorry," I said sadly, "but I don't know how to help you, Franklin. I don't know *what* yetis eat!"

I was sitting by my bed, twirling my spaghetti fork in my fingers as I pondered what to do. Franklin spied the noodles hanging between the tines and his nose twitched. His eyes widened and his thick tongue darted out, brushing his lips.

"What yetis eat!" he said, pointing to the fork.

I blinked.

"Huh?"

"What yetis eat!" he repeated, reaching for the dirty utensil in my hand.

I gave Franklin the fork and he lifted it to his nostrils, then he took a big whiff before he stuck it in his mouth and licked it clean.

"Mmmmmmmm!" he said with a huge smile.

"You like spaghetti?" I asked.

"Yes!" he said, bouncing up and down and shaking the floorboards. "Spaghetti! Franklin like spaghetti! YETI LIKE SPAGHETTI!"

"Sam, is that you?" called Dad from downstairs. "What are you doing? I said you could have a snack, but now you have to go to bed!"

"Shhhhhhhhh!" I hissed, putting a finger to my mouth. "Hold on, and I'll see if I can find some pasta for you. But you have to be quiet! You can't let Mom and Dad know you're really here!"

"Yeti like spaghetti! Yeti like spaghetti!" Franklin whispered, shuffling from foot to foot with excitement.

"It's just the monster," I told Dad as I went to the kitchen one more time. "He's really hungry tonight!"

Mom and Dad laughed.

"The monster can have a little more to eat, because I know he's growing a lot right now," said Mom. "But he also needs his sleep."

"Of course," I said, before I got several cans of spaghetti and returned quickly to my room.

Chapter 7 – Pasta la Vista, Baby

Well, can you guess what happened next? Franklin gobbled all the canned pasta down, then he demanded *more!* He was so happy, I couldn't help but smile, too. He was like a giant, furry baby, giggling with delight.

"Franklin like spaghetti! YETI LIKE SPAGHETTI!" he kept repeating, over and over, louder and louder when I wouldn't go back to the kitchen. And like a baby, the only way to keep him quiet was to feed him.

Finally I had no choice except to do what he wanted, otherwise he would have woken up the whole neighborhood—even with the storm raging outside.

"Oh, alright!" I said. "Just please lower your voice!"

Back and forth I went, sneaking up and down the stairs, retrieving canned spaghetti until long after Mom and Dad were asleep. Then, when we were out of canned spaghetti, I had to make fresh noodles for Franklin until his stomach was swollen and almost bursting.

And still he kept eating!

Canned pasta, fresh pasta, and even dried pasta—the yeti didn't care if it was cooked or not, or if it had sauce or not, as long as it was spaghetti.

He ate and ate, until finally the snowstorm outside my window began to die down, and the heavy gray clouds parted to reveal the pink glow of the sun rising on the horizon. Our pantry was bare. It was almost morning. I had school in a few hours. And I was *tired!*

Thankfully, so was Franklin.

"More . . ." the yeti mumbled, burping and licking his orange-stained lips.

"There isn't any," I told him truthfully. "You've cleaned out the entire pantry."

"More . . ." he insisted.

I shook my head and crossed my arms, unable to do anything else for my demanding visitor. "Nope," I chuckled. "Pasta la vista, baby!"

With his belly full and his eyelids starting to flicker, the abominable snowman sank to his knees and rolled under my bed, and soon his soft snores drifted out from beneath my mattress. I flopped down and closed my eyes, not even worrying about the gigantic mess I would have to clean up later.

The last thing I remember before I fell asleep was hearing someone whisper *"Thank you, Sam."* But I wasn't sure if it was the yeti or my imagination. Then I slipped into a deep, dark slumber.

The next day, I woke to Mom shaking me gently. She was standing over me, pointing with disbelief to the stacks of cans, boxes, and dirty plates on the floor.

"Goodness, Sam! How much did you *eat* last night?"

"It was the monster," I muttered.

"Is that right?" she asked. "The one under your bed? He must have had a monstrous appetite!"

I nodded, then before I could stop her, she dropped to her knees and peeked under my mattress.

"No, Mom! *Wait!*"

I expected her to scream when she saw Franklin, but she didn't. She just stuck her hands under my dangling blankets and pulled out a pile of grubby dishes.

"School has been canceled today because of the snow," she said. "So you can stay in bed a while longer. But make sure you still have breakfast when you get up."

Then she kissed me on the forehead and left.

I waited until Mom shut my door, then I sprang out of bed and searched for Franklin everywhere. I looked in the closet, behind the curtains, under my bed . . .

But he was *gone!*

The only thing reminding me of the yeti's visit was a small puddle of water on my windowsill, and a faint, tomato sauce footprint that was four times as big as my own by the door. I wondered if Franklin had been nothing more than a dream—maybe something I imagined after I ate all that food in my sleep. And I felt a bit sad at the thought.

I shuffled to my dresser to find some clothes, then I heard a tap on the glass of the window behind me. I looked between the curtains, but all I saw was the endless white of snow stretching forever. Then two giant black dots appeared, blinked and vanished, then materialized again.

Eyes! *Yeti eyes!*

"Franklin!" I cried with joy. I ran over and threw open the window, and the giant woolly creature pulled himself up over the edge into my room.

"Sam!" he replied, throwing his arms around me.

In the bright light of morning I noticed he wasn't so much an abominable snowman as he was a snow*boy*. Even though his shaggy head almost touched the ceiling, he was about my age. And when he stepped back and we stared at each other, I saw something else.

He was still afraid.

"Are you okay?" I asked.

"Franklin need to hide!" the yeti said, glancing over his shoulder at the snow outside. "Franklin scared!"

He looked at my bed and pointed to the narrow space underneath.

"Sure," I shrugged. "You can stay as long as you want."

Then the yeti smiled and slipped to the floor and gently eased himself under my mattress.

"Spaghetti for yeti?" he called out when he had made himself comfortable.

I grinned and got dressed, then went downstairs to see what I could find. I didn't know what Franklin's story was—where exactly he came from or what was chasing him, but I definitely knew what he liked to eat!

Epilogue

It's been almost two months since Franklin the yeti came into my life the night of the big snow storm, and we've already become best friends.

He sleeps under my bed during the day and goes outside for a while at night when he thinks it is safe, and we hang out together in my room when nobody is listening. He's great at hiding when adults are around, and he's getting really good at video games! I'm teaching him how to speak English and play the guitar, and he's starting to tell me a little about his home far away.

So far, I don't understand much. Something about big mountains, lots of ice, a cave where yetis live . . . and men looking for monsters, who kidnapped his parents one night when he was asleep. That's all I know. But I'm sure I'll get the rest of the story soon.

Meanwhile, I'm happy having a new pal who is always glad to see me. When I get home from school, Franklin almost leaps out from under my bed to greet me.

"Yeti love Sam!" he calls, giving me a big hug. Then it's "YETI LOVE SPAGHETTI!"

And that's my signal to fix lunch, which we share on the floor in front of my TV. I don't mind, because I love spaghetti, too.

Almost as much as I love Franklin.

About the Author

Hart Lee Serious is an author/illustrator with a seriously silly sense of humor. With a pen in one hand and a sketchpad in the other, he spends his days writing jokes, riddles, and stories to accompany his crazy cartoons so he can make super silly books especially for YOU!

Made in United States
Orlando, FL
21 December 2024

56328892R00019